Stitched Together

Stitched Together

Above the Rain Collective

2023

Above the Rain Collective
abovetheraincollective@gmail.com
North Georgia, USA

Contributing Editors:
J.A. Sexton

ISBN: 978-1-7377970-8-1

julietrose.author@gmail.com
authorjulietrose.com

Cover graphics and interior/exterior formatting by J.A. Sexton
Original cover photographs by Alois Wonaschuetz and Hans
Above the Rain logo artwork by Bee Freitag

To Lizzy, who always believes in me,
even when I don't believe in myself

"Normal is an illusion. What is normal for
the spider is chaos for the fly."
Charles Addams

Chapter 1

I n small towns, everyone notices when a new structure is being built. It becomes a focal point, a part of daily discussion over coffee and around shop counters. They conjecture the possibilities. What could it be? Will it create jobs? Will it change things? The older folk usually don't want things to change. For the younger people, they hope it's a sign of the future. They pray it *will* change things. Something new geared toward culture and growth. Something that recognizes their existence in the town and maybe will make them want to stay after they graduate. A place to break the monotonous day-to-day life they can't escape. Progress.

Most times it isn't, though. It's another mediocre business, mimicking all the others in town. The older residents grumble about growth but are secretly pleased their way of life isn't being challenged. The youth grumble about the lack of growth and are frustrated nothing ever changes.

The building sprouting up next to the only gas station in Daniels, Tennessee was nothing different. At first, when the metal girders went up, the teens in the area got excited. A pizza place? An arcade? A store that sold something other than cheap, shapeless clothes made for the elderly? Their minds were abuzz, imagining what it could be. Everyone had a different idea.

A few months later, after the windows and doors had been installed in the nondescript structure, they were disappointed when a sign for a sew shop appeared out front. A sew shop? More grandma stuff? Of course, it was. The youth didn't matter, after all. They were nothing more than a nuisance. Meant to be seen and not heard. Really, not even seen. Certainly not to have a say in a town that wasn't truly theirs.

This was the point of contention between the four teens sprawled out on the curb of the gas station, eating snacks and staring at the flat beige sew shop.

"I mean, seriously, how much business can that get, am I right?" Wes, one of the boys, said as he tossed a pebble across the parking lot.

It bounced across the asphalt and landed a few feet from the new parking lot of the sew shop. He took a swig of soda and peered back at the girl, Clare, sitting next to him. She nodded and squinted her pale blue eyes at the building.

"My mom says it's because old people are the majority here and have nothing else to do." She pushed her wavy, golden hair out of her face and shrugged. "They rule everything. Always have, always will."

Wes snickered, then tipped his head. "That they do. When we moved here, I had no idea I'd be stepping back to the fifties. It's so fucking boring here. I like you guys and all, but man, I wish we'd never set foot in this place. Every day drags on and on."

"Yeah, well at least you weren't born here. We've been bored out of our minds since our first breath," his buddy, Eli, joked. "I can't wait to leave as soon as I can. Go anywhere but here."

Leave. Wes thought about it every day. His family moved to Daniels the previous year when his mother became principal of the middle school. In a town of around three thousand people. His father could work anywhere as a tech consultant for online companies, so he was fine with wherever they went. Why did they choose this rinky dink town with nothing going on? They moved from Chattanooga and things were just fine there. There they blended in, here they were *that* family. The *black* family. His parents said it was because they could afford a house in Daniels and wanted something to call their own for once in their lives.

Something worth working for.

That much was true. They'd moved from a two-bedroom apartment to a five-bedroom, two-story Victorian with gingerbread molding or some crap like that his mother went on and on about. His parents were delighted and spent their free time restoring the house to its former glory.

Wes, however, was not thrilled. He missed his friends back home, even though he'd made a small group of friends there. Eli was the first. He and his girlfriend, Brianna. They'd plopped down next to Wes one day at lunch and asked him his name, Eli brushing his straight, deep brown hair out of his face and introducing himself to Wes with a handshake and a grin. Brianna smiled shyly, a petite, red-headed girl with soulful, gray eyes. They were the first to do more than give him weird stares and whisper behind his back. From that point on, he and Eli talked every day and played video games after school.

Then he met Clare in art class. She was a weird one, drawing pictures of zombie children. That made him like her. Not *like*, like her. Just as a friend. He wasn't a hundred percent sure Clare even liked boys. She never showed any interest and usually had her face in her sketch pad, drawing demented images. Even so, when he said hello to her, she immediately began rattling off obscure facts about the town, the people, and the history, which like much of the South was focused on how odd people were. Wes wasn't sure much of it was true, but Clare told the stories with such gusto, he didn't care either way. It was entertaining.

Eli got up and took Brianna's hand. "We gotta go. Brianna has piano class and I need to drive my Bubbe to the grocery store over in Price for a few specialty items for dinner. I promised her I'd be home shortly. You need a ride home before I go?"

Wes shook his head. "Naw. I'm going to hang out for a bit, then head downtown to see what kind of trouble I can get into."

Eli laughed, knowing it wasn't much, and turned to Clare. "How about you?"

Clare glanced up from her drawing, then shrugged. "I think I'll tag along with Wes and see what trouble he's getting into. Could be fun. If I go home, I'll just have to do chores and homework. Nobody wants that. Especially not me."

"Fair enough. Call me later, Wes. Maybe we can get online and play some video games after dinner. I think you're one up on me, I need to take you down once and for all, dude."

"Will do, though you know you can't beat me, fool. Have fun at piano practice, Bri," Wes replied.

Brianna wiggled her fingers in the air and smirked. "You know it. Maybe these appendages will be my ticket out of this podunk town."

Eli and Brianna headed for his car as Wes turned to Clare. "Before we go downtown, you want to go over and peek in the windows of the sew shop? See what's going on in there?"

She set her sketch pad down and tipped her head. "What, so we can see what old people do in their spare time? Sounds terribly exciting."

"Come on. We can head to Pope's Burgers and Ice Cream Shop after. I'll buy you a shake." Wes stood up and stretched his back. He grabbed his skateboard and tucked it under his arm since Clare was on foot.

At that offer, Clare shoved her sketch pad in her bag, slinging it over her shoulder, and rose next to him. "Deal. I'm holding you to it."

They wandered over to the newly paved parking lot, which seemed much too big for a sew shop, and went up to one of the windows. Inside was pretty dull, the walls painted a dim yellow with construction equipment shoved along the wall. There were three large rooms, separated by a doorway in between each. As they went along the outside, peering in, it confirmed this shop would be of no interest to anyone under forty. Wes internally yawned with the prospect of a bunch of grannies sitting around making quilts. He hoped he never got to the age where he found such activities stimulating.

When they got to the last window, Clare cocked her head in confusion as she stared through the glass, her brows knitted in a frown. She pressed her hand against the glass over her eyes to get a better view.

"What the actual hell is that?" she asked as she waved Wes over.

He came up beside her and cupped his hand to block out the light. In the center of the room was a crudely drawn symbol in what looked like charcoal or ash. "Uh, I don't know. Maybe they were measuring something out?"

"That is not a measurement I recognize from anywhere. It looks like some kind of religious or ritualistic symbol. Don't you think so? See how it has points drawn around the circle?"

"I don't know. Yeah, I guess you're right. Like something out of a cheesy, nineties movie about a creepy cult. You think they're a cult?" Wes teased.

At this, Clare laughed so hard, tears pricked her eyes. "The cult of grandparents? Oooh that would be a good band name. I need to write that one down. I doubt it, though. It's weird, but maybe someone was just fooling around. You know, broke in and left that to scare the old people. Maybe even the construction workers."

That made more sense than a cult of grannies. Wes stepped back and checked his phone for the time. "You want to head downtown? We have about an hour and a half before everything starts to close up for the night. Can't be out after dark, you know?" he joked. That was another thing he didn't expect moving to Daniels. Nothing except the bars stayed open after dinner time.

"Right? You promised me a milkshake," Clare replied, eyeing him sharply to make sure he remembered.

"I did."

They paused at the sew shop road sign as they were leaving and Clare grimaced. The sign looked like a quilt, but something about it was off. Clare traced her finger along the center of the image where the lines appeared thicker, and it was like a second image inside the squares came to life when she did. She raised her brows at Wes as her finger dropped to her side. He stared at where her finger traced. He saw it, too. It had to be a coincidence. A shitty coincidence, but there was no way someone would put *that* image in a sign.

Clare watched him intently, then tipped her head. "It's strange, right?"

"Yeah, gives me the creeps. Let's just go," Wes responded. He led the way out of the parking lot and glanced back as they hit the sidewalk. There was no way it was intentional, but it was there plain as day.

In the center of the very colorful, benign quilt, the rows between the patches made up a symbol that if not viewed the right way might not be visible. But once seen, it couldn't be unseen by the brain.

Grandma's quilt had a swastika.

"We ask only to be reassured about the noises in the cellar and the window that should not have been open."
T.S. Eliot

Chapter 2

W es couldn't get the image out of his head. He lay
in bed with his head in his hands, staring at the
cracks in the ceiling. Did they not realize they
had that in their sign? Should he let them know, so they
could change it before they opened? They might think he
was crazy and laugh at him if he even suggested such a
thing. It wasn't obvious when glancing at the sign at first,
but if anyone stared long enough or light hit it at a
certain angle, they'd have to notice.

He and Clare had seen it within a minute.

Setting his resolve, he needed to let them know
what they saw in the quilt of the sign, so they could fix it
before the shop opened. He'd hate if a bunch of old
people were accused of something so horrible. He didn't
want them to make fun of him if he went into the shop,

so he grabbed a piece of paper out of his notebook and scribbled a quick note:

Hello Stitched Together, (the name of the shop, which he found slightly disconcerting but wasn't sure why)

I was walking past your sign and saw something I thought you might want to know about. I hate to tell you this but if you look at the quilt a certain way, you can see a symbol in it. A bad symbol. I think because of the way a quilt is with the squares and all, it probably happened accidentally but thought you'd want to know, so you could fix it before anyone else saw it. I don't even want to say what it is but know you'd want to know. The center of the quilt makes a swastika. Just thought you needed to know before it caused you any trouble.

*A concerned citizen (*he started to write his name at first but felt stupid and changed it)

Wes folded the paper and glanced at his alarm clock. It was still early enough in the evening if he went now, he could make sure no one was there to see him drop the note. Or snooping around after dark. Not wanting to go alone, he texted Eli to see if he was around and wanted to take a ride over there. Eli was the only one with a car and Wes didn't feel like skateboarding over to the shop.

Eli texted back immediately. "Dude, I'm sitting here in the living room with my parents and aunt, bored out of my mind while they go through photo albums and tell stories. You have something you want to do tonight?"

"Yeah. Can you come get me? I'll fill you in once you get here."

"On my way."

Wes sat up and tucked the note in his pocket. He fished around his desk for tape, then headed down the stairs for the door. His parents were playing cards at the dining room table, their nightly routine after dinner. His brother Deo was engrossed in a comic book as he lay on the couch, his feet resting on the arm.

His mother eyed him. "What are you up to? Are you leaving again already?"

"Nothing much. Eli is coming to get me and we are going to hang out for a bit. My homework is done," Wes replied, hoping they'd drop it.

"Stay out of trouble," his father said without looking up from his cards. "Be home by curfew."

"I will, Dad."

Wes darted out the door to wait for Eli on the street. He didn't have a reason he and Eli were hanging out and didn't want to be grilled by his parents for one. They trusted him but still wanted to know the who, what, where, when, and whys of everything, even so. Luckily tonight, they didn't ask.

Being such a small town, Wes didn't have to wait long for Eli to arrive as everything was pretty much within walking distance anyway. Eli drove up a minute later, his headlights blinding Wes for a moment. Eli rolled the window down, grinning.

"Thanks for the rescue, dude. Bri is out at a movie with her sister over in Price. I was stranded at home with nothing to do. Where do you want to go hang out? Nothing's open now. How about the reservoir?"

Wes showed Eli the letter and filled him in on what he and Clare had seen in the sew shop sign. Eli stared at him for a moment, then back at the letter. His face was hard to read, but Wes sensed something under the surface. Tension.

Eli put the car in gear and eased down the street. "You sure about this?"

"I mean, I think so. Clare and I both saw it. We can go look and you tell me," Wes replied, now unsure of himself. Maybe he was overreacting.

They drove to the shop and were surprised to see cars there. Like, a lot of cars. Eli pulled into the gas station parking lot, so they weren't obvious and stared over at the sign. At first, he seemed unconvinced, shaking his head, not seeing what Wes was talking about. Then as if hit with a bolt of lightning, he went rigid and sucked in his breath.

He saw it.

"What the fuck, dude?" he whispered and sat back in his seat. "Yeah, I see it now. That's so messed up. They can't possibly know about that, right? But how could none of them have seen it when the sign was approved for display? Someone had to have signed off on it. I don't know. Are you going to give them the letter with all those people in there?"

"I hadn't planned on it," Wes confessed. "I thought the place would be dark and empty at this time and I'd tape it to the door."

"Huh. Why do you think all that many people are there this late?"

"Maybe workers? Contractors?"

"On a Sunday night? I doubt it. You want to go over or wait til another time?" Eli asked.

Wes knew he'd lose his nerve if he waited. "Let's leave the car here and walk over. Maybe I can slip it under the door or something without being noticed."

Eli watched him, considering. Then he unbuckled and turned the car off. "Always down for a little investigating. Let's see if we can look in the windows and see what they are doing in there."

Wes felt his stomach drop, sensing they were getting in deeper than he intended. He just wanted to leave the note on the door and be done with it. He nodded, not wanting to seem like he was chickening out. "Probably a potluck or something."

They snuck up to the building, trying to stay in the shadows. The first two rooms were dark but the last room, the one he and Clare had seen the drawing on the floor, was lit up. They crept up to the window, crouching by it. It had a shade drawn but at the right angle, they could see into half the room. What they were seeing inside didn't make sense to either of them.

A group of older people were sitting on pillows. They were cross-legged and holding each other's hands. They were seated around the symbol on the floor with their eyes closed, each placed at one of the points around the circle. They were moving slightly from side to side and murmuring something neither Wes nor Eli could make out. It was like they were in a trance of some sort.

Eli looked at Wes, his face contorted in confusion, then shrugged in question as he raised his hands to his sides. Wes shook his head and peeked back through the slit. One of the old men was saying something as the others nodded in unison. Smoke rose from the symbol in the center and was beginning to take shape. Wes realized it was in fact some kind of ritualistic drawing and they were performing a ceremony of sorts.

The smoke in the center of the symbol evaporated all of a sudden and the people around the circle opened their eyes, frustrated. They stared around at each other and the man talking appeared angry. He threw his hands in the air, speaking harshly and pointing to where the smoke had been. He was saying something to the other people, who seemed ashamed.

Wes stepped back, feeling a heavy sense of claustrophobia washing over him. He wanted to do nothing more than leave the area. He almost felt like they were being watched by something around them. Not the people in the room, something else entirely.

A glance at his friend showed Eli felt the same. Eli was tense, his fingers digging into his arms and his back rigid. He stared at Wes, his eyes round and unblinking. What they'd seen was some sort of black magic, Wes was sure of it. Now, his joke about it being a cult seemed all too real and not so funny.

"Wes, this is bad news. They are fucking around with shit they shouldn't be," Eli whispered. "They could really do some damage if they don't know what they are doing in there."

Eli was right. Whether they were bored with retirement or purposefully trying to summon spirits, they were creating a situation that didn't have an easy out. Eli grabbed Wes's arm and pointed in. The ceremony was over and the people were beginning to stir, stretching out their legs and arms.

Wes knew they needed to move fast so they weren't caught staring in the window. He mouthed, "Let's go."

"Demons are like obedient dogs; they come when they are called."
Rémy de Gourmont

Chapter 3

As they stepped away from the window, the old people began to get up from their places and mingle about. A few grabbed their belongings and headed for the door. Wes panicked and threw the note at the door as they scurried away, not willing to be confronted by anyone after what they'd observed. It bounced off and landed on the welcome mat. He and Eli got past the windows and ran the rest of the way to the car as the door of the sew shop opened and people began to spill out. One of them spied the note and picked it up, frowning as she unfolded the paper to see what it was.

Wes and Eli climbed into Eli's car and watched as the woman read the note, her face twisted in confusion. She peered at the shop sign for a moment, then gazed around to see if she could figure out who'd left the note at the door. Not seeing anyone, she shifted her attention back to the note.

Wes and Eli acted as if they were just at the gas station hanging out and tried to not make it obvious they were watching her. The woman waved down a man passing her on the way to his car and showed him the note. He did what she did, first peering at the sign, then looking around for who left it. Before long, a whole group gathered around, reading the note. They handed it around from person to person, taking turns reading what was written inside.

What struck Wes the most was that no one seemed horrified or even surprised. They almost seemed delighted by it. Like finding the golden egg at an easter egg hunt. *Like they wanted people to know on some level.* He stared at the sign and fought back the same unease he'd felt when writing the shop name on the letter. Stitched Together. It made sense for a sew shop, however, it seemed to have a hidden meaning. Like the sign did. They knew there was a swastika hidden in the sign because they'd *put* it there in the first place.

A secret code. A message to others like them. Those that were stitched together. Like a gene strand or belief. He stared at Eli, who'd come to the same conclusion by the expression on his face. Eli fired up the car and backed out, not wanting to stick around any longer. It wasn't a sew shop, or not only. It was a meeting house. In their small town. Something the symbol had represented many years before in another country determined to eradicate select members of their community. A group of people who hated people who weren't like them. People like Wes and Eli.

They were silent on the way back to Wes's house. Both were horrified at the discovery and didn't know what to do with the information. Wes was glad he'd decided not to sign his name and out himself to the people there. Not that he could've known what they were really like. Eli pulled up in front of his house and cut the engine, letting out a heavy sigh.

He turned to Wes. "Dude, this is bad. Not only are they a bunch of bigots, but they're practicing some sort of black magic in there, I think. Calling something up. Did you see that smoke?"

Wes stared out the front window. "I did. For what, though? To do what with it?"

Eli rubbed his hand across his face as he thought. "Nothing good, that's for sure. My family has a history of dealing with this kind of hatred. I'm sure yours does, too. If they're trying to draw up beings from another realm, I'm guessing they aren't happy sitting around bitching about how their town has changed. They mean to do something about it. With some pretty fucked up help."

Wes gulped and felt his palms get sweaty. A bunch of decrepit old people couldn't do much by themselves, but what if they managed to get something else on their side? Something evil, demonic. He met Eli's eyes. "Are you thinking we need to do something about it?"

"Yeah, but what can we do?" Eli answered, a line forming between his hazel eyes.

"We could burn the place down," Wes suggested.

Eli tipped his head. "That's a start. But they'll just find a new place, eventually. This has been going on forever, in back rooms everywhere. We need to find a way to stop *them*."

That was true. However, it might slow them down enough to come up with another plan. Wes looked at the light outside his front door. His parents would never believe him if he tried to tell him what he and Eli saw. They thought this was a quaint, small town where they could raise their kids and retire. They had no idea how much they were unwanted there by some people. How willing those people were to get rid of them.

Wes shuddered. "It would be almost impossible to stop the people since they have existed forever. We don't even know how many people here are involved or who they all are. So, we need to undo what they have done so far. Close the door."

Eli nodded. "Yeah, I guess you're right. This is bigger than us, at least right now. So, close the door. The question is, what is it going to take to do that? Do you think the symbol is the portal?"

Their eyes met and they knew. They needed to break in and get rid of the symbol, maybe throw holy water on it or something. Then burn the place down. Wes put his hand on the door and pushed it open. He turned back to face Eli, not wanting to leave the plan hanging.

"I gotta go before my parents come out looking for me. I'm going to search some stuff up tonight on my computer. Try and figure out how to stop this. I'll text you anything I find out, okay? I think we may need to go in and see what we're up against. Talk to the old people there. See if we can fish anything out of them. For now, I need to find out if they can actually summon evil. Grandpa's demons." Wes wryly thought Clare would like that as a band name.

Eli tried to smile but his mouth grimaced instead. "I'll do the same. Hey, man, I need to tell Brianna. For my own sanity. I can't keep something like this from her. I trust her a hundred percent, though."

Wes shrugged. "Fair enough. I'm going to let Clare know what we found, too. She was the first one to see the symbol in the sign and the one on the floor. Plus, she is into some of this otherworldly shit. She might have some insights. The more of us on this side, the better. This is beyond crazy."

Eli looked like he was going to speak, then didn't. He set his mouth in a line and stared out the windshield into the dark. Wes understood. What they'd just witnessed was bizarre. Something out of a horror movie. Maybe the old people were playing with things they didn't understand and wouldn't get anywhere with it. They hadn't been able to complete the ceremony that night. However, Wes and Eli couldn't risk it. They needed to stop it before it became unstoppable. They'd require Clare and Bri's help, as well. They needed an army.

Wes waved at his parents as he came in and went straight to his room, not wanting to talk with them and possibly let on anything was wrong. They had a way of seeing through his moods and would sense something was up. He shut his bedroom door and flopped down on the bed, his heart still racing in his chest.

What had they gotten themselves into?

He texted Clare what happened that night, expecting her to tell him he was overreacting or tease him about being dramatic. Instead, she asked him where and when she needed to meet up with them to deal with it. It was that simple for her. She also told him not to go back as certain things could latch onto him if he was unprepared.

Come home with him.

Wes sat up and stared in the mirror, praying nothing had come home with him. He didn't look any different and had no sense of having company in the room with him. He worried about exposing his family to anything that might harm them. He lay back down and took a few deep breaths. He needed to let Eli know that as well. They'd taken a risk going there that night. Now, they needed to go back prepared for a fight.

He texted Eli. "Hey, Clare pointed out we may have been exposed to some things there, which might have followed us home. Do you feel anything weird on your end?"

Eli texted back. "It's always weird here, but outside of my parents slow dancing in the living room at almost midnight, no. I don't think anything came home with me. I've just been researching anything I can find on what we saw there. I haven't felt anything out of the ordinary, though."

"Okay, good. If you do, let me know. I don't sense anything here either but just to be safe, be aware. Have a good night, dude."

Wes texted Clare he'd let her know as soon as they had a plan. She texted back a thumbs up and he shut his phone. He needed to focus, to gather as much information as he could find. It was going to be a long night on the internet, trying to figure out what it would take to close the door.

"Everyone is a moon and has a dark side,
which he never shows to anybody."
Mark Twain

Chapter 4

The shop was devoid of people every time they went by for the next couple of weeks. Work was clearly being done to finish the building and the inside space was starting to fill with sewing machines and the accoutrements required for sewing. As any plain old regular sew shop would have within its walls. Nothing seemed out of the ordinary in the space, but there was no doubt they were using the shop for nefarious reasons. For an intent which had nothing to do with sewing. Something was hidden within the walls and the people.

Eli and Wes drove by numerous times during the week after the workers left for the day, but the shop stayed dark and unattended. Maybe the old people had given up after their failed attempt. If so, burning down the shop seemed a bit extreme and dangerous.

After a few weeks, a grand opening sign was placed out front and Eli and Wes doubted what they saw was more than a messed up, senior citizen séance.

What they did notice was when they were downtown, it seemed like old people were watching them. Teens always drew stares from the older community but this was different. It was like their movements were being tracked. Or maybe they were just paranoid because of what they saw, however, more than once they caught the stare of one of the elderly in the community. When the teens went to greet them, the older person turned and walked away without saying a word. It was strange. No one knew they were outside the shop that night, so there was no reason to be garnering this kind of attention.

On the opening day of the sew shop, the four friends swung by after school to scope the place out. The first room was filled with all kinds of sewing gear from needles to thread, patches, fabric, and the sort. Not to mention stuff none of them knew what it was. The second room was set up as a sewing classroom and a few people were at sewing machines, demonstrating how to make a rag quilt out of scraps of fabric. The third room, the one with the symbol on the floor, was sealed tight.

"Should we ask about it?" Clare questioned, wiggling the door handle which didn't budge. They didn't have time to consider the question when they were approached by an old woman who very much resembled

Mrs. Claus. She was even wearing a red blouse. She smiled brightly at them and waved around the room they were in at the rows of sewing machines.

"Are you young people interested in learning about sewing?" she asked, her eyes twinkling. She really did look like Santa Claus's wife from books and movies when they were kids. In an eerie, horror movie way.

Wes cleared his throat and smiled. "No ma'am. I mean, maybe. Do you teach classes for teens?"

She winked. "We could. None have ever asked. What would you like to learn? Do you have any experience with sewing?"

At this, Wes faltered. He didn't know the first thing about sewing. Brianna came to his rescue and pointed toward the people sitting at machines. "Are they making rag quilts? My grandmother used to make those for us when we were little kids. Before arthritis made it too hard for her to cut fabric. I'd love to learn how to do that." She emphasized the word *love* and smiled sweetly.

"We sure could teach you that. We don't have any classes planned currently, but check back in a month or so, once we've had time to set our schedule," the woman replied, an effective brush-off.

Clare, not one to be brushed off, placed her hand on the door handle of the third room again and met the lady's creepily friendly stare. "What's in this room? More sewing machines?"

The woman glanced at the door, then back at Clare's face, never breaking form. "Oh, you know, storage, that kind of thing. The mess we keep from the public eye. Maybe one day we will get organized and be able to open that space for something more useful."

Nothing about the woman set off alarm bells, yet everything did. As if Santa Claus has a Mrs. Claus robot he sent in to eat babies. She waved them toward the first room and tipped her head in a grandmotherly kind of way. "Come on back to the front. We have cookies and tea set out for guests. You can enjoy some while I take down your names and contact info for upcoming classes."

Wes met Eli's eyes and shook his head just barely. No way in hell were any of them leaving their contact information. Eli made a quick judgment call and pretended his phone was vibrating. He put it to his ear and put a finger up toward the lady. He carried on a one-sided conversation, then hung up.

"Hey, guys, we gotta go. My mother is hung up at work for a bit and needs me to get my little sister from gymnastics." Eli didn't have a sister.

The woman, still smiling, nodded her head, then placed her hand on Brianna's shoulder. "Oh, what a shame. All of you?"

Eli shook his keys. "Only one with a car, unfortunately. Thank you for your hospitality. We'll check back about those classes in a while."

The four of them practically tripped over each other getting out the door before the woman had a chance to say anything else. As they were leaving, Wes noticed the woman who'd found his letter standing at the back of the room, watching them. She had no friendly smile, no North Pole hospitality. Her eyes were sharp and knowing. She seemed particularly focused on Eli, making Wes's skin crawl. He pushed his friend forward out the door, not looking back.

They clambered into the car and Eli's hands shook as he stuck the key in the ignition, missing the first time. "What the fuckity fuck? Did you all feel that gust of cold air while we were leaving? Made the hair on my neck stand up straight."

No one else had and Wes knew why. The lady at the back of the room had marked Eli. Eli Schwartz. From one of the only Jewish families in town. Wes felt a wave of nausea come over him and rotated his hand in a hurry-up fashion, wanting to leave as soon as they could.

"Dude, just drive. I want to get the hell away from here as fast as possible," he stammered out.

As they backed out of the sewing shop, the lady who'd found the note came to the door and watched them leave. Her face was twisted in a smirk and she lifted her hand in a wave. Not a friendly kind of wave. More of an *I know who you are* kind of wave. Eli faltered for a second, goosebumps forming on his arms. Wes felt it this time, too. He clapped Eli on the shoulder and squeezed. They needed to move fast.

On the drive home, no one spoke at first, processing the experience they'd had when Clare practically yelled out of the blue, "Well, that was fucking weird!"

"No lie. Whatever they're doing there, they're up to something sinister. It may look like a sewing shop, but that's clearly not all that's going on," Wes agreed. "That lady who came to the door when we left was the one who found my note. I have a feeling she knows it was us who left it. Knows we know."

"So, now what?" Brianna asked, her voice small.

Eli shifted in his seat, pressing his foot to the pedal to put as much space as he could between them and the shop. The car strained with the added pressure, but Eli didn't let up. He gripped the steering wheel, his knuckles turning white. It almost didn't sound like him when he spoke. "Now, we need to bury them."

Eli was typically the rational one and never got heated or showed anger. They all stared at him and the venom coming from his words. He was right. It wasn't over. Mrs. Claus and the rest of them were up to no good. More than no good, they were up to something evil. No one else around seemed to comprehend the danger, so it was up to the four of them to take care of the situation.

"We need to go back," Clare said.

"Today?" Bri asked, reaching out for Eli's hand. Eli met her eyes and grasped her hand in his.

"No, we need to figure out when they're holding their little meetings and figure out exactly what it is they are conjuring up," Clare replied.

"Eli and I have been driving by, they haven't been doing them," Wes explained.

"They wouldn't unless it was on a certain cycle. Like a lunar cycle or something like that. We need to figure out when they are performing them," Clare explained, tapping her chin as she thought about it.

Eli slowed the car and glanced back. "The last one was a full moon. I remember because it was so bright. My Bubbe was telling me about a prayer on the full moon."

Clare sighed and pressed her hand against the glass of the window, peering up at the sky. "Let me look at this book I bought at a metaphysical shop in Price and see if there is some symbolism to full moons and conjuring up spirits. In the meantime, keep driving by to see if they are there at night."

Wes nodded and wondered what they'd do if the old people were there. Break in and demand them to stop? Call the police? It all seemed so unreal. His mind went back to the lady's eyes as they landed on Eli, the hatred he saw there. He didn't know what they'd do, but he knew it was on them to do something.

To stop what was coming.

"Believe nothing you hear and only one
half that you see."
Edgar Allen Poe

Chapter 5

"Look at this," Clare said as she shoved the book from the library across the table. "It says to conjure a spirit, or whatever, you need to pick the right time, place, and create a 'welcoming' atmosphere. Weird, right? It sounds like they picked a full moon, and were creating an atmosphere conducive to calling up a ghost or demon. But do you think the shop itself is built in a designated place? I thought it was strange it was next to the gas station but nothing in this town makes sense anyhow. It's all haphazard, however, I wonder if they didn't pick that spot for a specific reason."

Wes peered at the book Clare was showing him. Everything they could find for research was pretty tame. Or so out there it seemed too far-fetched to get actual information. The people from the sew shop seemed to know what they were doing. Enough, anyway, to get something to pass through. None of the books they found explained exactly what they'd seen the old folks doing. What he and his friends did know was the people had a symbol on the floor, they were sitting in a circle holding hands, and murmuring or chanting as they rocked side to side. The man seemed to be casting some sort of spell and the others were going along with it. Then, there was the smoke that came out of nowhere.

Wes shoved the book away and sat back in the chair at his dining room table. His parents were still at work, so he and Clare were reading through the books they'd been able to find. The internet had gone off in too many directions, making it hard to determine what was real and what was made up. It was like there was too much information but not enough to actually help them form a plan. He groaned, rubbing his face.

"I feel like we are going down a rabbit hole, Clare. And a scary one at that. I don't want to open anything we can't close or that might put us in danger. Put our families in any harm."

Clare finished writing notes and peered up at him. "What's the alternative? We can pretend none of this happened and maybe for a while things will seem normal. Wes, those people won't stop. I saw how that lady looked at Eli... looked at you. Do you think they will get bored and move on anytime soon? Or ever? This has been going on for centuries, you know? People using things to help them perpetuate hate and hurt others."

Wes sighed and pulled the book back toward him. "I suppose not. I just don't know what can help and what can hurt. My little brother is about to be home and I don't want him telling my parents what we're doing with any of this. He's nosy as hell. Can we take this back up later over the phone?"

Clare nodded and began slipping the books into her bag. "Sure. We're running out of time, though. The next full moon is in a couple of days and if that's when they're doing their ceremony, we need to be prepared to stop it until we figure out how to close the door. They may succeed this time, then what? It's easier to take down a bunch of old people. A lot harder to take down some demonic entities."

The front door swung open and they could hear Wes's little brother throw his backpack down and stomp through the house toward the kitchen. They quickly shoved the rest of the books in Clare's bag and stood awkwardly by the table. Deo walked in and stared at them side by side for a moment, then shrugged with a smile forming on his face.

"Were you making out or something?"

Wes felt his face get hot and stared at Clare who smirked. She slung her bag over her shoulder and cocked her head. "Wes isn't my type." She headed for the door, then spun and met Wes's eyes. She raised a couple of fingers and gave him a hard stare. "Two days."

Wes nodded and glanced at Deo who was rummaging in the cabinet for a snack, having moved on from anything to do with them. He gave Clare a thumbs up, feeling stupid for having done so. She gave a dramatic wink and left. He turned to help Deo get cookies out of the upper cabinet and poured them each a glass of chocolate milk.

Later that night, the four friends met online and went over any research they'd gathered. What they did know is that the symbol acted as a doorway to another world. The full moon made the spell the people were casting stronger. The group of them coming together helped conjure whatever it was they were trying to summon. The rest was up in the air. They still didn't know how to close the door. They agreed to go to sew shop on the full moon to see if that's when the people gathered. If they were there, the plan fell apart at that point. Confront them? Observe and wait?

"We need to break them up, stop them before they finish the ceremony," Clare insisted, her large eyes staring at them through the screen.

"How?" Eli asked.

"However we can. Break a window, blow a horn. Just enough to keep them from focusing enough to get the portal open. Or more open since it seems they've cracked it already," Clare responded, moving her hands in a circle to represent to opening.

"The portal?" Bri replied, frowning at Clare's gesture. She hadn't seen the symbol or the ceremony.

"Portal, doorway... whatever they're opening in the symbol to let things pass through," Wes explained.

"Got it," Bri said, though she seemed like she didn't understand.

"Okay, so we'll go there and when they start their mumbo jumbo, we do something to stop them. A distraction. How do we know they won't be able to ignore it, or just go back to what they were doing? How do we know whatever they're evoking won't come after us instead?" Eli questioned.

Clare shook her head, then put her hands in the air. "We don't."

They agreed to meet on the evening of the full moon. Wes and Clare were going to arrive early at sundown on foot to scope things out. Eli and Brianna would come once it was dark with the car, so they could make a quick escape if things went awry.

Wes turned off the computer and went to bed. Part of him wanted to tell his parents, to let them take the burden off him. The other part knew they wouldn't believe him and might even try to stop them. He closed his eyes and couldn't get the one lady's eyes out of his mind. It was like she was seeing right through them. Like she knew what they were up to and could read their minds. He rolled over and clicked on the radio. He cranked up the music, closing his eyes. He moved his head side to side to the rhythm, trying to shut the image out.

His mother came to the door and knocked. "Hey, hon, can you turn that down a little or put on headphones? We're about to turn in for the night."

"Sure, Mom," Wes replied, wishing he could tell her. He slipped a pair of headphones out of the side table drawer and plugged them in. His mother smiled and gave him a small wave as she headed to her room.

The next morning, he decided no matter what it took, they needed to stop whatever was happening at the shop. To protect his family, to protect the town. He met Clare walking to school and matched her steps. Neither spoke as they made their way down the sidewalk. She glanced at him and nodded. They were all scared. Even though she always showed a tough exterior, Wes could see she was worried about what might come.

By the night of the full moon, they'd met and discussed their plan so many times online, at school, and after, it almost didn't seem real. They acted out different scenarios, various escape plans. Like practicing for a school play. A life-or-death school play.

Clare came home with Wes after school the day of the plan and they sat in his room "studying" until it was time to leave. He left his door open so his parents wouldn't suspect he and Clare were doing anything other than test prep. Even so, they walked by way more than was necessary. He was relieved when it was time to go and told his parents he was walking Clare home and meeting up with Eli for a soda at the gas station. Deo made kissing faces as they left, but Clare didn't seem to notice.

They made it to the gas station before nightfall. Sure enough, as they suspected would happen, car after car pulled into the sew shop parking lot. One by one elderly people climbed out, heading for the door. Balding men and round ladies, dressed in their polyester shirts and muted slacks. Looking like they were going grocery shopping on a Wednesday morning, not about to open the gates of hell.

Once they all moved inside the building, Wes messaged Eli and told him to park on the far side of the gas station, so they wouldn't be seen. Clare was already moving to the side of the sew shop, ignoring Wes whispering for her to stop and wait for the other two. Wes had no choice but to follow and caught up with Clare hiding in the shadows on the other side of the building. She put her finger to her lips and pointed to the partly uncovered window. Wes crept over and peered in, shocked at what he saw. He took a step back, trying to process what was happening inside.

Eli's car eased into the gas station lot, parking around the far wall. A moment later, Eli and Brianna snuck over and Clare waved at them to show where they were hiding. They joined Wes and Clare and the four of them huddled around the edges of the window to see in. If they had any doubts before about what was truly happening, what they saw in the room pushed those aside. Wes watched, not believing what was transpiring.

What at first looked like a church social, everyone greeting each other with a smile and a handshake took a disturbing turn. Each person walked up to the man who'd been talking the first time. They were smiling and extending their hands. He grasped their hands and nodded, a smile frozen on his lips. He wasn't shaking their hands, though.

As he grasped each of their hands in his own, he drew out a knife and sliced their palms open.

"Hope not ever to see Heaven. I have come to lead you to the other shore; into eternal darkness; into fire and into ice."
Dante Alighieri

Chapter 6

They watched in horror as one at a time the old folks went up to have their palms cut open, then retreated to their spot on the floor. Wes recognized the pharmacist, Mr. Bedlam, move to sit next to one of the town librarians, clenching his bloody hands in his lap. They smiled at each other as if they were passing on the street on a sunny afternoon. Wes recognized others in the room but couldn't remember their names offhand. He only knew Mr. Bedlam because sometimes his mother sent him over to pick up Deo's asthma inhalers. Mr. Bedlam was always nice, even joking about things. Nothing about him seemed off. Until now.

Once all the people were sitting around the symbol, the man who'd been slicing their palms took the bloody knife and placed it on a pile of fabric in the center of the symbol. He moved to his place between two others and they all clasped hands, some wincing from the pain of the wounds. Wes noticed something on top of the pile of fabric under the knife and squinted to make it out. His stomach clenched in fear when he realized what it was. His note. The note he'd left about the sign. Why did they have that there with the other things?

The people began to sway and murmur like they had the previous time Eli and Wes observed them. The man started to chant again, louder this time, more confidently. Clare squeezed Wes's arm and pointed to the center. Smoke began to rise through the fabric. It twirled up toward the ceiling and thickened.

"What the hell is happening?" Brianna whispered, her voice terrified. Eli wrapped his arm over her shoulder, drawing her close to him. Brianna looked away from the window and buried her face in Eli's arm.

"Old people have gone and lost their friggin' minds," Eli whispered back.

The group sitting around the circle's voices got faster and their sways became almost rhythmic, picking up to a frenzied pace. Like a choreographed dance. The quicker and louder they chanted, the more formed the smoke became. Much more than the previous time Wes and Eli had seen it.

"Should we do something?" Eli asked, stress making his voice tight with worry.

"Not yet, I don't think," Wes answered. "We need to see exactly what they're doing first, what their intent is, so we know how to stop them all together."

It didn't take long for them to see what was happening as the smoke became thick enough to start raising the fabric off the ground. Except, it wasn't just fabric. As the smoke took form within it, they could see it was a uniform of some kind. An old, faded military uniform it appeared like.

All of a sudden, Clare gasped and pointed at the figure in the uniform. It now took the shape of a man, but that wasn't what she was gasping at. On the sleeve of the uniform was a black and red band. In the center of the band was a white circle with a black swastika dead center. The friends looked at each other, Eli's face draining of color.

"That's a Nazi officer's uniform," he whispered faintly. He wavered and braced himself on the window frame with his free hand.

They peered back in and smoke was no longer there, now stood a specter in the uniform, grinning and holding the bloody knife the man had left. In his other hand, he held Wes's note. The people around the circle opened their eyes and were still chanting. The more fervent they got, the less translucent the soldier became. He gazed around, satisfied, at the old people as they gave him strength and power through their words and actions.

"We need to stop this, NOW!" Clare exclaimed and took a step back away from the window.

Wes looked around for a rock or something they could throw through the glass. Not seeing one, he ran to the door and began pounding on it with all his might. The other three ducked down past him and headed toward the gas station. Wes ran back to the window and saw the group had scattered and the apparition was no longer standing there. Just a pile of empty clothes in the center of the symbol.

Members of the group were going for the door, so Wes hunched down and ran behind the building to hide. He crouched down, looking for a route behind the gas station to get to Eli's car. He could hear yelling as the front door flung open.

"Who's there?" a man's voice boomed with fury through the darkness.

Wes held his breath. They'd surely come around back, searching for the intruder. If he ran to the gas station they'd spot him and being one of only two black boys in town, they'd know who he was. He bolted into the woods and peered over to the gas station. He couldn't see the rest of his friends and hoped they made it to Eli's car safely without being spied.

Lights began to bob through the woods, so he moved as fast as he could through the trees until he got to the highway, then ran down the road away from the shop.

Car headlights came up behind him and he knew he was caught. He tried to act like he was just out taking a stroll, but he was breathing heavily and stumbling. He heard the car slow and panicked, thinking about jumping down into the ditch to hide.

"Dude, it's us. Get in the car!" Eli's voice cut the fear paralyzing Wes and he whipped around to see Bri waving at him frantically from the passenger seat. He froze for a second, hearing people moving behind him in the woods.

"Come on, Wes! They're getting in their cars to come this way. Move!" Clare spat as she flung the back door open for him.

Wes dove into the backseat with her as Eli peeled out before the back door even closed all the way. They sped down the highway, then veered down an unlit dirt road. Eli kept turning down roads until they were well off the main road. He pulled to a stop, cut off the car, and put out the lights.

They sat in silence for long enough to know the shop people would've passed them by. Wes leaned forward, staring out the window to the pitch black. No one was coming.

"Did they see you leave the gas station?"

Eli shook his head. "I don't think so. A few people were leaving the gas station at the same time, and I went in the opposite direction of the sew shop. We played it cool, going the speed limit and all. I looped around and came back, following some other kids in cars on the strip. That's when we saw they were searching in the woods and some were getting in their cars, as well. We passed them but no one really looked at us. Just a couple of kids out killing time, driving around as always, I guess."

"Okay, that's good. We need to talk about what we saw, however, I'm about to be late for curfew and can't afford to get grounded right now. You guys want to come over to my place? We can put a movie on in the basement, so my parents leave us alone. I'll make some popcorn and we can come up with a plan to stop them. This is way bigger than I was expecting."

"Yeah, no shit," Clare whispered. "If we hadn't stopped them tonight, we might not have been able to. We do need to go back by and see if they are back at it, though. There isn't another full moon for a bit but they definitely had some new tricks with the uniform, blood-binding, and all. Now, I don't know if they'll need the moon anymore. Any natural light may work."

"So, you are saying they could do this again tomorrow night?" Bri asked.

"I think so. Their skills have gotten much stronger. They could go back at it tonight if they really wanted to, but I think Wes pounding on the door may have interrupted the flow for now, if you get my meaning. They'd have to start all over and it might not work."

Wes tipped his head. "Like the ghost thing won't come back because I disrupted the focus?"

"More or less, but let's go back by anyway. Just a few teens out killing time, right?" Clare responded.

"They had my letter in the pile," Wes remembered out loud. "I don't know what for, but that thing was holding it when it took shape."

"Why would they use that?" Bri asked.

"I really don't know, but it freaked me out," Wes confessed. "Like they know it's from me and are tracking me now."

Eli turned on the ignition and flipped the headlights on. Wes noticed Eli looked like he had tear tracks on his face. Eli wiped his face and cleared his throat as he pulled back out onto the road. Wes reached out, placing his hand on Eli's shoulder.

"You alright, man?"

Eli met Wes's eyes, his own hard and determined. "Yeah, I am. I'm just ready to go kick some Nazi ass."

"When there's no more room in hell, the
dead will walk the earth."
George A. Romero

Chapter 7

They made their way into the basement after brief small talk with Wes's parents. Deo tried to tag along with them, but Wes beseeched his mother with his eyes to stop his little brother from pestering them. She smiled, snapping her fingers.

"Hey, Deo, come help me make some popcorn. Dad and I are going to watch Pet Sematary tonight. You can watch with us if you'd like."

Deo eyed the retreating teens, then turned to his mother. "Really? You never let me watch scary movies with you."

"You're twelve now, I think we can change the rules a bit. Just as long as you don't try to climb into bed with us tonight 'cause you're scared of ghosts and ghouls coming to get you," she teased.

Deo straightened his back and sniffed, indignant. "I don't get scared, Mom. I'm not a baby."

A look passed between the two adults and they hid their smiles from their younger son, who most definitely still got scared. His mother stood up to go to the kitchen and waved her hand at him.

"Come on, then. You can melt the butter, while I pop the corn."

Wes paused at the basement door, watching the exchange between his mother and little brother. He remembered being Deo's age and trying to convince himself and everyone else he didn't get scared anymore. After tonight, he could say without a doubt, he still got very much terrified.

Eli peered up the stairs from the down in the basement. "Wes, you coming?"

"Yeah, sorry, got distracted."

Wes thumped down the stairs to the half-finished basement his parents deemed could be his hangout space if it meant they could get control of their television back. It had an old couch and a couple of chairs around a beat-up coffee table, plus a television and a small fridge for cold drinks. Eli sat next to Brianna on the couch and Wes and Clare sat across from each other in the chairs. Clare took out a sketchbook and began scribbling out what they'd seen in the shop. It was too real. Even her drawing gave Wes the creeps.

"Okay, so we need to act fast. If they don't need to wait until another full moon to evoke spirits, then we can't wait either," Wes said, still watching Clare sketch out the Nazi soldier. "We can't fight an army of monsters or whatever is coming."

Eli sat back, holding Bri's hand in his. "We can go back tomorrow night. You can say you're sleeping over at my house, Wes, so you don't have to worry about curfew. But what if they're already there when we get there? Are we supposed to take out elderly people from our town? That might get a little messy."

Clare glanced up. "They deserve it. Bigots."

Eli nodded. "I'm not saying I disagree, but stopping a ghost is different than harming a flesh and blood human. We can go to prison for that. Besides, I don't think any of us have that in us. Killing someone."

"We can go to prison for burning down a building also, right?" Bri chimed in, pointing out that no matter what they did to stop it, they were putting themselves at serious risk.

Wes shrugged. "Only if they catch us. We can make it look like an accident."

Clare sighed and threw her sketch pad on the coffee table, the Nazi specter glaring back at them from the page. They all stared at the drawing and knew time was running out to make a decision. Whatever they were going to do, they needed to do it sooner rather than later.

Wes picked up the drawing and bit his lip. How could they fight something that wasn't really there? Or worse, what if it was?

"Tomorrow night it is. Since they didn't go back tonight, maybe they'll lay low for a few days. Let their wounds heal before having to get them sliced open again," he said, referring to the cuts on their palms.

Clare raised her eyebrows. "Good point. They got pretty deep cuts and being as old as they are, probably lost a fair amount of blood tonight. That might buy us some time. *Might*."

"Eli, can you drive by tonight on your way home and make sure it looks like they still haven't gone back?" Wes requested.

Eli seemed uncomfortable but bobbed his head. "As long as I can stay in the safety of my own car on the road. I'm not going up there alone."

They hashed out a few more details, agreeing they needed to find a way to burn the place down without it being traceable. None of them had any clue what that might be and were too afraid to research on their computers. Wes said he'd go to the library the next day after school to see if he could find any books that might offer a solution.

After popcorn and a movie, Eli and Brianna rose to leave. Wes and Clare got up, as well, and the four stood awkwardly. They knew the next time they were all together, they were taking on something much bigger than any of them, even combined. Clare closed her sketchbook and slid it into her bag.

Eli laughed nervously. "Alrighty then. Guess we'll see you tomorrow at school, Wes. Clare, you want a ride home with us?"

Clare grabbed her pack and nodded. "Thanks, I'm a little spooked to walk home alone."

"You know if Clare is spooked, we're in trouble," Bri said, trying to bring a little levity to the moment. No one laughed.

"Yeah, I think we need to all stick together from this point forward to be safe," Eli responded.

Wes walked them to the door, noticing the rest of his house was quiet and everyone was in bed. Now that his friends were leaving, he kind of wished his parents were still awake. He watched the three of them head to Eli's car from the front window.

Eli stopped and raised his hand to Wes. Wes waved back, their eyes sharing a secret message. He'd only known Eli a year but he was already one of the best friends he'd ever had.

They all were.

Wes brushed his teeth and peeked in on Deo, who was reading with a flashlight under his blanket. He tapped on the door. "You aren't fooling anyone under there. You know that, right?"

Deo poked his head out, the flashlight casting a ghoulish shadow on his face. "Not trying to, I like how it feels. Like I'm in a cave."

Wes walked over and sat on the edge of Deo's bed. "I used to do that, too. Felt like my secret space. Did you like the movie?"

"It was cheesy."

"Most Stephen King movies are. The books are better," Wes offered.

Deo climbed out and sat cross-legged on his bed, watching Wes. "Mom won't let me read the books yet. She said I need to wait til I'm fourteen for those. She said they are scarier than the movies."

Wes nodded, that was probably true. "Hey, this weekend, you want to go downtown to the comic book shop and look at game cards?"

"With you?" Deo asked, surprised.

"No, with the boogeyman," Wes teased, then immediately regretted it, knowing maybe the boogeyman *was* real. "Of course with me."

Deo cocked his head, trying to see what Wes was playing at. "Okay?"

"Seriously, little bro. Just you and me."

Deo's face brightened and he grinned. "For real? Just you and me."

Wes rubbed Deo's head and got up. "Go to sleep. Morning will be here before you know it."

As he walked to his room, that statement hit home. Morning would be there before they knew it and it brought the biggest fight of his life. One he wasn't sure he was ready for. At least he had his friends on his side. It wasn't much but it was something.

It took hours for sleep to come and when it did, Wes felt like he was slipping between layers of existence. Flashes of the ceremony kept popping up. He couldn't get the dead eyes of the Nazi specter the old people had conjured up out of his mind. The way the soldier looked like he'd been waiting a long time to come back to life. Eli said the uniform was an officer's uniform.

Which meant there *was* an army coming.

"By the pricking of my thumbs,
something wicked this way comes."
William Shakespeare

Chapter 8

The four friends met up the next afternoon, armed with very little. The internet knowledge they'd gathered was mostly rhetoric and opinion. Wes brought bags of potato chips since he read they could be used to start a fire in a survival book, due to their high-fat content and they'd leave no trace behind. Clare brought vials of holy water she stole from the church, the irony not lost on her as she poured some into each of the small bottles for all of them to carry on their bodies.

Eli made them individual amulet pouches to wear around their necks, which as far as Wes could tell were filled with a combination of plants, rocks, herbs, metal, spices, even string. Brianna brought pennies from the town fountain, saying they still held good luck from people's wishes.

Wes's family didn't have any superstitions or good luck tokens but he brought a few silver rings his grandmother handed down to him before she passed, figuring maybe she was watching over them. As she'd watched over Wes when he was a little boy. The ragtag group put together their collection into the pouches Eli provided and strung them around their necks.

It was easy to tell themselves this was all make-believe and perhaps they were a little too eager for an adventure, but Wes reminded himself he saw smoke coming from a symbol. Not a container of any kind. Forming out of nowhere in the center as the people clasped hands. Then they all saw a Nazi officer develop right before their eyes. Worst case scenario tonight, they'd get caught and get in serious trouble for breaking in. Best case scenario, they stop whatever was being started... and not get caught. He hoped in either scenario, they burned the place to the ground.

The group rode in Eli's car until they were within sight of the shop. It was dark and the parking lot was empty. That was a good sign. They needed to make sure to close the doorway the old people opened with their ceremony before burning the place down. Otherwise, it might remain open forever and let who knew what through. Maybe they could get in, cast the spell Clare found in one of the books to close other spells and thus the door, remove the symbol, then set the place ablaze without anyone noticing them. Burning the building stopped the people at least temporarily, closing the portal stopped the other beings from passing through into this world. Both were equally important to complete.

After parking the car down a dirt road, they skirted through the trees to get to the back of the shop. They inched around the front, careful to not be seen by anyone at the gas station. No witnesses to identify any of them. Wes stopped and put his hand up as they rounded the corner, making sure they were truly alone.

"We need to check to see if any of the windows or doors are open," he whispered.

Clare nodded and began checking the ones near her. Everything was locked up tight. Eli and Bri went around the other side of the building but came back shaking their heads. No luck. Wes tried the door near him which was also locked.

On the last window, he clasped the amulet and said a little prayer, though he didn't know to whom. He reached out and grasped the bottom of the window, pushing up with all his might. It slid open so fast it almost slammed against the top of the frame. Eli caught it before it hit the top and made any sound, drawing attention to their presence at the shop.

"Dude, you'll get us all caught before we even have a chance to do anything wrong," Eli joked, though his face was dead serious.

One by one, they climbed through the window, shutting it partially behind them. Enough to look closed to the naked eye, but leaving it cracked so they could make a quick exit if needed. They made their way through the dark rooms until they came to the last one with the symbol on the floor. Wes eased the door open. To their surprise, a single candle burned in the center of the crude drawing, and Wes felt his heart pounding in his chest. The candle appeared freshly lit, having barely burned down at all.

Was someone there?

They immediately retreated into the dark doorway and scanned around the room. It seemed empty, even though the candle continued to flicker brightly. They hadn't seen anyone leave in the time they'd been outside. How could that be?

"I think they left a light burning to keep the door open. That way they wouldn't need to do so much to evoke spirits," Clare explained, pointing at the candle. It seemed dangerous to leave it burning, however, clearly safety wasn't the priority for the shop people.

"How is it still burning?" Bri asked, confused. The candle didn't look burned down at all.

"I'm guessing they put a spell on it to not burn out. As long as the doorway is held open by it, the candle won't burn down and the flame won't be extinguished," Clare responded.

"So, are we able to put it out?" Wes inquired, wondering what it would take to break the spell.

If they couldn't put the candle out, they couldn't shut the door. The whole point of coming there was to close the portal. If they couldn't do that, burning the place was pointless.

Clare shrugged. "Your guess is as good as mine. It doesn't look like anything has come through so far. Maybe if we can blow it out after we cast the spell, the door will close. All we can do is try at this point."

Eli moved along the wall toward the symbol when something shot out of the candle at him. An orb. He jerked back and stared at the glowing light. It danced in front of him, almost like it was reading his presence as he stepped back away from it. The ball hovered close to him and began to take shape.

At first, the shape was nondescript, but as it came closer to Eli, it took a more human form. Arms and legs unfolded from the blob, then a head began to rise from what was becoming shoulders. Eli was frozen in place, unable to move away from the form in front of him. He was being held captive by its presence.

To their astonishment, a soldier, a different one than last time, began to appear in front of Eli, his uniform reminiscent of a different time. A darker time. Somewhat like the one the old people had left of the symbol during their previous ceremony, but not an officer's uniform. This time around the specter came with its own uniform and didn't require one to be left to summon its presence.

That meant the magic was more powerful than before and they were in serious trouble. As the swastika started to form on the being's armband, Eli was forced to his knees and blood began to run from his eyes. He cried out in pain, unable to escape. Bri ran toward Eli, placing herself in between the apparition and her boyfriend. This broke the trance and Eli rose, pulling Brianna beside him. He clasped her hand as they attempted to get away from the demon.

The apparition grinned, its mouth spreading almost comically across its face as it raised a bayonet at the couple and moved with force toward them. Eli grabbed Bri and threw them both on the ground as the bayonet hit the wall, digging a deep hole in the drywall. The soldier moved above them, its hand raised to strike again, having corned them on the ground. Clare screamed to try and divert the soldier's attention. The creature faltered and the pair scrambled across the floor past it to get back to the doorway.

Just as they made it back to Wes and Clare, more lights shot out of the candle, filling the room with forming shapes. Like before, the lights developed into Nazi soldiers, each carrying a weapon of some kind. These weren't merely ghosts or apparitions, they were demonic forces coming to finish a battle they'd lost long ago. To seek revenge.

The demons now were developing a physical form, one that could create real harm. If they left the walls of the sew shop, they could open wounds barely healed over from the war and destroy everything in their path.

"Fuck, what do we do now?" Eli asked, never letting go of Brianna's hand.

Wes held his breath, not sure what they could do. He shook his head, wracking his brain. "We need to shut the fucking portal. Somehow."

The doorway was open and they were quickly getting outnumbered. With each passing second, more and more orbs of light were passing through the candle, then becoming part of the ever-growing army. Wes wondered why these orbs didn't start releasing until he and his friends entered the room. That's when he realized, the dark forces needed something to latch on to. Evil needs a victim to carry out its intent. The soldiers needed a mark to bring them forth to kill. It gave them purpose and purpose gave them power. That was why the old people had used his letter in the previous ceremony. To create a connection to a real person.

Like coordinates.

Clare began to recite the spell she'd found to try and close the door before any more entities came through the portal. Wes wrapped his fingers around the amulet and ran toward the center of the room, hoping to kick over the candle and stop the incessant flow of evil being released from its light.

As he entered the symbol, he felt his strength being sucked out from his body and fell to his knees in an attempt to catch his breath. It was as if the wind had been knocked out of him and there was no way to recover from the blow. No air entered his lungs no matter how hard he tried to breathe in. His muscles gave out and he couldn't move, even to escape.

He could hear Clare calling to him but he couldn't turn around to see her. The candle was still too far out of reach and he felt an overpowering need to sleep. A strange sensation came over him and he felt like he was no longer part of his body, like he was being eviscerated. As he saw the figures of soldiers with their weapons raised coming for him, Wes fought the urge to close his eyes. He attempted to yell for his friends to run but no words came forth from his throat. His breath was gone and he was being taken under.

At that moment, he felt something grab his foot. He tried to scream, his mouth agape with no sound. He kicked as hard as he could to get free, which was little more than a muscle twitch. Whatever had him, was dragging him back and he had nothing left to fight.

"The monsters that rose from the dead,
they are nothing compared to the ones
we carry in our hearts."
Max Brooks

Chapter 9

W es turned his eyes and saw his friends had made a human chain to reach him, pulling him slowly back across the symbol to an area outside of the lines. Once he was clear of the charcoal outline, Wes felt his strength return and got up painfully, retreating to the nearest wall to put his back against. He caught his breath and tried to shake off the weight that had been taking him down inside the circle. He was convinced he would've died had his friends not stepped in to save him.

The room was now full of Nazi soldiers and they were descending upon the four friends. The group gathered together in a huddle, clutching their amulets. It seemed to offer some protection, but not enough against the sheer number of beings coming toward them with weapons raised. They needed to find a way to escape but they didn't know how and the candle continued to let more soldiers through.

"They're stronger than us, there's no way we can hold them off... much less stop them," Clare whispered, her eyes darting toward the looming forms. They were trapped with nowhere to run, all escape exits being guarded by the Nazis.

"Maybe. Or maybe we need to stick together. I mean, they're just ghosts, right?" Wes responded, not convinced of that fact. Whatever they were, they were more than whisps and shadows.

"I don't know, Wes. Ghosts can't stab you with bayonets," Eli replied.

There was no denying that fact. One of the soldiers had driven its bayonet at Eli and Bri, leaving a large and jagged hole in the wall. These soldiers were real in their own way. It appeared they could physically accost the four of them and do real and lasting damage.

"What if we go in together? Like a wall. If we walk toward the candle as a group, maybe we can reach it. We can depend on each other's strength," Bri suggested.

It was worth a shot. The friends eyed each other, then clasped hands. They moved toward the stream of apparitions, hoping they were strong enough to take on whatever was coming for them. As they came toe to toe with the soldiers, Wes could hear loud ringing in his ears. He could tell his friends heard it, too. They wouldn't be able to communicate as they went into the symbol. The forces at play were using every trick to stop them from extinguishing the candle.

They pushed on, feeling like a thousand winds filled with shards of glass were pushing back on them. Their skin burned and rivulets of blood ran down their arms and legs. They heard screams and moans, children crying, wails of suffering. The soldiers were stabbing them, their blades making wounds, though their amulets seemed to be creating some sort of buffer to prevent them from being killed. However, the pain was very real and it was hard to continue on. Every time one of them fell to their knees, the other three lifted them back up to their feet. They were willingly marching into hell and were being made to pay dearly for it.

Wes closed his eyes and held Clare's hand tighter. The friends pulled together, joining their arms at the elbow to not lose their grip and pressing together to reduce the amount of flesh the soldiers could injure. It was like playing Red Rover against the devil. Whatever was there wanted to drive them apart, so it could break them down and stop their progress.

The nearer they got to the candle, the harder it was to move. Wes could feel the force trying to rip Clare away from him but refused to let go. The only way was to hold on. Just when he thought the forces would win, the wind stopped. They could still see and sense the storm around them but they were in a vacuum. No sound, no movement happened around them. Wes loosened his grip on Clare and glanced around.

The four of them were in the eye of the storm, standing by the candle which gently flickered like a prayer candle at church. It seemed almost vulnerable, a simple breath would extinguish the flame. However, the candle was protected by some kind of bubble. They couldn't knock it over or blow it out.

Eli paced back and forth, twisting his hands together. "Nothing about this is what it seems. There are so many layers. We are sitting ducks now and this stupid fucking candle is mocking us. We could die here."

A soldier leapt at them and was sucked into the flame, disappearing from their world. All around them were the angry faces of the Nazis, waiting for them to exit the eye so they could consume them. The soldiers couldn't enter the eye and the friends couldn't leave. Wes glanced at Eli who shook his head, exasperated. They were safe but they were also trapped. Clare knelt by the candle, reaching out. Her hand hit an invisible force.

"Now what?" she whispered as if she were speaking to the candle itself.

The rest of the group stood frozen, unsure of what to do when Wes remembered watching the old people sitting in the group with their hands clasped in unity. They'd opened the door by doing that, by creating a rift in reality through the connection between them. A bond of shared hate and bigotry. Aligning their beliefs and their souls opened the portal, allowing demonic beings to escape. Beings who also aligned with their beliefs. They'd used black magic but it was more than that. They'd come together with a shared goal. They were even willing to maim themselves to reach that end.

Wes and his friends needed to do the same but in a different way. With a different purpose. He motioned for them to sit down in a circle around the candle. They reached out and grasped hands, closing their eyes but nothing happened. Clare tried the spell again and while the flame flickered, it continued to burn. Even if they cut their palms and pressed them to each other's, they knew it wouldn't reverse what had been done. It wouldn't shift the power of the original spell. Besides, they were all already bleeding.

None of them had the ability to close the door and even in coming together, they were helpless to bring about change. Wes stared around at the symbol on the floor, then at the soldiers waiting to pounce. He thought about the old people coming together to summon these monsters. Some who could barely walk on their own. Others that spoke in the halting, tired gasps of the end of life. Weakened by time.

How did they manage to gather such force when they hardly had any strength? To create a strong enough doorway to allow the demons of hell to pass through? In turn, how could he and his friends create a force strong enough to fight against the other one? To stop the army of Nazis waiting to destroy them.

Wes stared at the candle. A simple little flame that had so much capability. Or did it? Was the flame merely a reflection of that which lit it? Instead of trying to put it out, should they be trying to shift its energy to a different kind of power?

An image came to Wes of when he was a little boy, sitting with his grandmother on her back porch. They were shucking corn for dinner and she was telling him about how when his father was little, he liked to pretend the corn cobs were race cars. He'd attach round pegs as wheels to the cobs and roll them around the kitchen.

This always made Wes laugh, picturing his father as a little boy playing with corn cob cars on the kitchen floor. It made him see his father differently. Not just a grown man with a job and lots of opinions about how Wes should live his life. So serious all the time. His father had once been like him. Young and funny, full of imagination.

Like Wes and Deo.

Wes shook his head. Why was he thinking about that memory when the forces of hell were breathing down their necks? He glanced around at his friends, fear lining their faces as they pressed as far away from the soldiers and their weapons as they could. They needed to come up with a plan and fast before they ran out of time. Wes went back to the memory, turning it over in his head. There was something there he needed to understand.

What did his grandmother or his father have to do with any of this? What was his grandmother trying to show him? The memory seemed important but he didn't why. Then, as if a secret was whispered in his ear, he knew what it meant. What he needed to do.

He began to speak.

"Even the dead tell stories."
Marcus Sedgwick

Chapter 10

"My people were forced to come here from another land to serve white people. Scores of them died on the journey. They were enslaved for many years and suffered greatly at the hands of those who saw them as less than human. As property. My family rose out of that suffering and decided to fulfill their true destiny in a country that wasn't their own. To make it their own. My great-great-grandmother on my father's side was the first to be born out of slavery. My grandmother on my mother's side was the first in her family to go to college. My mother and father bought a house here in Daniels that once my people were not allowed to step foot in, except as servants. They have taught my brother and me that nothing is beyond our dreams. That we belong anywhere we want to be and no one can tell us otherwise.

Through their determination, I witnessed this to be true. I intend to follow in their footsteps," Wes told his friends, pride swelling in his chest at his family's strength and perseverance.

As he spoke the candle flame grew in length and leaned toward him. When he finished speaking, the candle flickered and dimmed slightly. The others saw this transformation and understood what needed to be done. The soldiers seemed to have faded in their intensity, though they still stood guard outside the eye of the storm, waiting to attack.

"My family came from Ireland," Bri said softly. "They were poor and when they arrived here, no one would give them work. They were spit on and called names. Told they were dirty, unworthy. They were forced to work for almost nothing and lived in crowded buildings where sewage ran across the floors. Disease among the Irish in America was rampant. My great-grandfather was one of only two survivors out of seven children in his family. The rest died from illness and starvation, some as only babies. He was determined to make it better for his children and built his house with his own hands, using materials he scavenged and bartered for. My parents taught me to love and respect all people, and that no child deserves to die because of something someone else has to easily share. They always say 'what's mine is yours'. I intend to carry on in their footsteps."

The candle flame arched toward her and the apparitions began to fade a little more. The eye around the candle grew larger, pushing back the soldiers.

Clare cleared her throat and glanced around at her friends. "I don't know much about my family history. We are white, we've been here forever, I guess. I don't really know, my family doesn't talk about it. My story is my own to tell. When I was younger, people would tease me about who I'd grow up to marry. It was such a thing. In school, at family gatherings, everywhere. Like that was my purpose in life. Which boy would take my hand and define me? I didn't know what they meant or how I should feel about it. I mean, I didn't feel that way. I didn't want to marry any boy. Or anyone. Not now, anyway. I know if the time comes, it won't be a boy, though. That's not who I want. For now, I want to make my own path. Define myself. I want to walk in my own footsteps." She smiled and met her friends' eyes. The candle wavered, reaching out for her, then retreated into a smaller flame, its strength diminishing.

The soldiers were now transparent, desperate to get to the four friends. A few rushed at them and immediately were absorbed by the flame of the candle. The friends watched in horror, hearing screams coming out of the dying light.

Their eyes shifted to Eli, who was staring down at his lap, his thin shoulders tense and stiff. They all knew they needed to tell their truths to shift the power of the light to take away the soldiers' strength and close the door. Eli peered up at them, his eyes filled with pain.

He wiped a tear and shook his head. "I don't want to do this. To tell of what my family went through during the Holocaust. I hate this. These monsters," he waved his hand around the room at the specters, "they almost made sure I wasn't here. They murdered most of my family. My grandmother only survived because she was a baby and was smuggled out in a sack of dirty laundry. Her mother had to give her over to strangers to try and save her life. She gave up her only child because there were people who would murder a baby because of its genetics. She did save my grandmother, but every other member of the family was tortured and killed during the Holocaust. My grandmother's parents, their siblings, cousins, *all* of them. Even the smallest of the children. My grandmother was raised by a family in England and she came here after school where she met my grandfather while working in a hospital. She only learned of her family through stories from survivors and what little records she could find that hadn't been destroyed. They had no footsteps left for me to walk in." Eli began to sob, his face pressed to his hands.

Each of his friends came around him, forming a new circle of light. Eli was the candle and his friends were helping him by openly offering their own light. The flame in the candle grew large and dragged the remaining entities into its light, filling the area with the most horrible, deafening sounds as they were consumed by the fire. With the shift of focus away from evil, the candle in the center of the symbol went completely out. The storm was gone and the room left empty.

The friends glanced around, waiting for something else to pop out at them. When nothing did, they rose and began rubbing away the ceremony symbol in silence. When the drawing was nothing more than smudges on the floor, the friends stared at each other. Wes nodded at Eli and handed him matches.

"We'll knock the candle over and set this bitch ablaze. People will think the crazy old people and their ceremonies did this. You want to do the honors?" Wes asked, squeezing Eli's shoulder.

"More than you will ever know, dude," Eli answered with gratitude.

To ensure the place went up, they tipped over cans of paint thinner they found left in the space. Eli took the matches, then lit the candle, watching it for a moment. Now, it was just a candle but it still had power to do something that needed to be done. Eli kicked it over, catching the floor on fire, which quickly spread to the nearby walls.

Eli, Bri, and Clare climbed out the open window, while Wes took the bags of chips and set them on fire in the other rooms to make sure the fire took everything. A few matches was all it took. The building burned so fast, it was as if it was meant to go.

The four friends retreated to the woodline and watched the structure get eaten by the flames and disappear into the ground. Firetrucks roared up within a few minutes, but it was too late. The Stitched Together sew shop was no more. The tired teens made their way back to Eli's car through the woods so they wouldn't be seen. They sat in the car with it off for a moment, the reality of what just happened sinking in. They'd closed the door. The people and their hate still existed but they'd managed to stop them for now.

Wes turned to Eli, then to Clare and Bri. "No one gets to take our world away. No one. This is our time and we get to make the rules. Whether they like it or not, we are the ones writing history now."

Eli fired up the car and dropped everyone off at home. Eli stopped in front of Wes's house last and let the car idle. The two boys didn't speak, letting the words from earlier be enough. Tonight they'd grown from being friends to being brothers. A lifetime bond that could never be broken. Through their shared commitment to equality, they'd defeated evil. Wes climbed out, then turned back to Eli, his voice strong and true.

"We walk together."

"Silence encourages the tormentor, never
the tormented. Sometimes we
must interfere."
Elie Wiesel

Chapter 11

Word of the fire spread around town almost as fast as the fire itself had consumed the building that night. As the friends hoped, it was chalked up to a candle left burning around flammable chemicals. Nothing remained but a pile of rubble on the scorched earth. It became a sight of interest and speculation, with locals stopping as they went by to say what a shame it was. Not that any of them cared about a sew shop, to begin with. It was simply something else to talk about.

None of the shop people said too much. Some disappeared in the night as if they'd never been part of the town. Maybe they hadn't because no one seemed to miss their presence. When the others were asked if they'd rebuild, they shrugged and said they didn't have any plans to at the time. They pretended to be devastated about the fire or perhaps they were devastated... just not about the building itself. They still showed up at community gatherings and acted as if they cared about those around them, all the while holding hatred in their shriveled hearts.

Within a few months, vegetation began to crop up around the barren earth and was allowed to flourish, burying the remaining debris of the shop. Soon, the sew shop was all but forgotten and the locals went on to fresh gossip and old complaints. Wes and his friends didn't forget, though, and kept their eyes out for any new buildings cropping up, in the off chance the sew shop people decided to rejuvenate their plan. They also observed the people they knew to have been part of the ceremonies, knowing they were still making plans and wouldn't stop until evil prevailed.

Sometimes, each of the friends would get a strange feeling, like they were being watched. Most times, no one was there when they turned to see. However, every now and then, they'd find one of the shop people eyeing them from afar. Their dead eyes calculating the teen they'd seen. Each of the four friends knew they needed to get out of town, also knowing it wasn't over for anyone left there. However, there was nothing more they could do as long as the group stayed behind the scenes. It was a waiting game that could last decades. It had before. It would again rise up when no one was suspecting.

One day, after Wes got his first car, he took Deo for a drive. They went past the empty lot and on to the reservoir. Wes parked the car and they hiked out to the other side where almost no one went. Deo was now fourteen and Wes was about to graduate from high school. They sat at the edge of the water on a wooden bench, staring across the expanse.

Wes turned to Deo. "You going to miss me?"

Deo grinned and shrugged. "Maybe a little."

"I need to tell you something before I go. Something really important."

"Okay?"

Wes rubbed his chin as he thought. "You need to never be afraid to stand up for what's right. To speak the truth and fight for others. Even if it's hard, even if you are scared to do it."

"I know," Deo replied as if this was old news.

"I mean it, D. If something doesn't seem right, it probably isn't. It's up to you to call it out. Do you understand what I'm trying to say?"

"Okay," Deo said, softer this time.

"Since I'm going off to college, I need you to keep an eye on things here. If anything seems off to you, let me know right away."

"Off like how?"

Wes knew he needed to tell his brother a little more to get him to understand. "My friends and I burned down the sew shop a couple of years ago. It wasn't an accident. We did it on purpose."

"You did what?" Deo asked, his eyes wide with shock that his brother could do such a thing. Wes never got in any trouble.

"We had to. There were... uh, bad things about that place. Really bad, like evil things." Wes knew it sounded like bullshit, but he didn't want to scare Deo too much either. "We did it to save people, D. I promise we were doing the right thing."

Deo peered at Wes's face to see if he was pulling his leg. Some devious big brother prank before he left for college. Seeing Wes was dead serious, he sat back. "What exactly am I looking for?"

Wes considered this, it could be almost anything, anyone. "You'll know when it happens, you'll just get a strange feeling or something won't look right. They hide in plain view."

"They?"

"There's us and there's them. We're on the good side, the right side. They could be anyone. Don't assume because they act nice or look a certain way, that they're good people. Even people around here who seem nice to your face can have dark secrets. See people with your gut, not your eyes."

Deo nodded and stared out over the water. He trusted his big brother and Wes was talking to him like a man, not a boy. They'd always been close but now he felt like Wes was his friend as well as his brother. He sighed. "I wish you weren't going so far away, Wes."

Wes put his arm over Deo's shoulder and pulled him close. "Not so far away. You know where to find me. Just pick up the phone and reach out if you need me."

The call came a couple of years later. Wes was heading out of class for the day when his phone lit up. Deo was calling in the middle of the afternoon, which wasn't like him. Wes put the phone to his ear. "Hey, little bro, what's up?"

"You gotta come back home as soon as you can, Wes. Something is going on." Deo's voice was strained and he sounded scared.

"Are Mom and Dad okay?" Wes asked, worried. He'd spoken to them the night before and they seemed alright then.

"Yeah, they're fine. It's not that. It's something else. Like we talked about before you left for college," Deo explained.

Wes stopped dead in his tracks and shifted his backpack to his other shoulder. *Like they talked about before.* His heart began to beat faster. "That day at the reservoir?"

"Yeah, that day. They put up a new building where the sew shop used to be. A vacuum store."

A vacuum store? Those didn't exist anymore, did they? No, they didn't, and certainly not a new one in this day and age. That was a bad sign. Enough years had passed and people moved on. It would be easy to start again without anyone thinking twice about it. Wes knew Deo wouldn't overreact and probably held off calling to make sure.

He sighed and considered his options. "Anything else to note?"

"The people there are weird. They were staring at me and my friends at the gas station when we were hanging out. Watching us the whole time. They were scowling, well most of them. One lady looked like Mrs. Claus on drugs," Deo said, then chuckled like he felt stupid for saying it.

"Fuck. I gotta go, D. I'm coming home. Now. Stay away from that place and those people. You did good. I'll see you soon," Wes promised, his brain immediately forming a plan.

He hung up the phone and dialed his other brother. It rang a few times and Wes was afraid he wouldn't reach him in time. "Come on, come on," he whispered into the phone.

When Eli picked up, Wes was relieved to hear his friend's voice. They'd gone to school a thousand miles away from each other but were always connected. Same with Clare and Brianna, who'd each gone their own way after high school. Bri to school on a music scholarship, though she and Eli maintained a long-distance relationship to the day. Clare chose to travel around the country, working on farms to pay her way.

It was time to bring them all back together. They had work left to do.

"Wes! Good to hear your voice. It's been a bit. I've really missed you. How's school going?" Eli asked, his voice hinting he knew more was coming.

"Hey, dude. It's time."

In moments betwixt the deepest dreams
A powerful shadow lurks unseen
It hides in stories and make-believe
Gathering followers in between

Upon waking, it's dismissed as fear
While gaining limitless strength
The sun rises to shine unaware
As the penumbra expands in length

To bear on and deny existence
Is to feed the insatiable beast
It grows within apathy and hate
Devouring those who fight the least

Stand up my brothers and my sisters
For now, the hour to resist is nigh
Yea, the monster has come a'calling
And will leave the murdered where they lie

Acknowledgments

Thank you to all my readers, beta readers, and reviewers for your constant support and feedback. Thanks, Leigh Kenny for your words!

To my children who entertain even my craziest of ideas and are willing to offer constructive criticism to help me make the best story possible.

To my soul sister, Lizzy Johnston, who convinced me this was worthy of a novella when I sent her the short story. She pestered me into it.

To Justin who begrudgingly understands when I say I need to write, I NEED to write and will be cranky until I do.

To all the teachers who encouraged me to write from an early age. It mattered.

To my family who reads my books even when they probably don't want to.

Books by the author:

Novels:

Do Over
We Don't Matter
Prick of the Needle
Through the Surface
Trigger Point
Carrying the Dead
Catch the Earth
In Dreams, We Fly

Anthologies:

Summer Slasher Horror Anthology
Books of Horror Anthology 4 Part 1

authorjulietrose.com